The power of
Po /

DREAMWORKS

KUNG FU PANDA 3

The Power of Po

adapted by Maggie Testa

Simon Spotlight

New York London Toronto Sydney New Delhi

SIMON SPOTLIGHT
An imprint of Simon & Schuster Children's Publishing Division
1230 Avenue of the Americas, New York, New York 10020
This Simon Spotlight edition December 2015
Kung Fu Panda 3 © 2015 Dreamworks Animation LLC. All Rights Reserved.
SIMON SPOTLIGHT and colophon are registered trademarks of Simon & Schuster, Inc.
For information about special discounts for bulk purchases, please contact Simon & Schuster Special Sales
at 1-866-506-1949 or business@simonandschuster.com.
Manufactured in the United States of America 0116 LAK
2 4 6 8 10 9 7 5 3
ISBN 978-1-4814-4105-6 ISBN 978-1-4814-4106-3 (eBook)

It was an awesome morning in the Valley of Peace that could only be made more awesome by some awesome kung fu training with Master Shifu! But the day got less awesome when Po and the Furious Five learned that it would be Shifu's final class. From now on, Po would be in charge.

Po was nervous. What could he possibly teach the Five? But Shifu hadn't given him a choice, so he started giving instructions.

"Monkey, Immovable Mountain Stance," Po ordered. Monkey did as he was told, only to end up falling straight down to the floor. *Thud!*

"Tigress, Tornado Backflip," Po continued. But that wasn't the right call either, and Tigress twirled directly into a ball of fire. *Hiss!*

Then Po accidentally caused Viper to fly into Crane, and then they both fell on top of Mantis.

"Ow, my claw thingy," Mantis moaned. Soon the Five were a tangled mess on the training room floor. Po's first day of teaching was not going well for anyone.

Po found Shifu meditating before the statue of the great master Oogway. Po told Shifu he didn't want to be a teacher. But Shifu told Po that teaching was his next step, just as Shifu would also be taking *his* next step—from teacher to Master of Chi. Po didn't know what chi was, and Shifu explained that chi is the energy flowing through all living things.

"But there's no way I'm ever going to be like you," said Po.

"I'm not trying to turn you into me," replied Shifu, walking away. "I'm trying to turn *you* into *you*."

As Po pondered Shifu's words in the mortal realm, Master Oogway was face-to-face with his old enemy, Kai, in the Spirit Realm. By stealing the chi of every kung fu master there, Kai had become very powerful. Kai battled Oogway, stole his chi, and turned him into a tiny jade amulet, which Kai wore around his neck.

Now Kai was strong enough to leave the Spirit Realm. Kai and all the kung fu masters whom he had turned into jade amulets set off to find Master Oogway's students to steal their chi too!

Meanwhile, Po was at his father's restaurant trying to absorb all that Shifu had told him. Po had thought he knew who he was, and now suddenly he didn't. It was all very confusing. And that's when he heard even more distressing news—a stranger was about to beat his dumpling-eating record!

"100, 101, 102 . . . ," the customers were chanting.

"103!" finished the stranger, his mouth full of food.

"Who are you?" Po asked.

"I'm Li Shan," the stranger replied. "I'm looking for my son. I lost him many years ago."

"I lost my father," Po told him. "I hope you find your son."

"I hope you find your father," Li answered.

Mr. Ping and his customers couldn't believe how much Po and Li looked alike—their bellies even jiggled the same way! But neither Po nor Li realized it until . . .

"Son?" asked Li.

"Dad?" asked Po.

"Well, don't just stand there," said Li. "Give your old man a hug!"

Po was ecstatic to be reunited with his panda father. There was so much catching up to do!

But first, Po and the Furious Five had to defend the Valley of Peace. Kai's jade army had arrived.

"They are some kind of Jade Zombies," observed Tigress.

"Jombies!" Po and Monkey said at the same time. "Jinx!"

As he was fighting the jombies, Po began to recognize them. Each was a legendary warrior . . . but from hundreds of years ago!

"Your chi will soon be mine," they said at the same time. And then suddenly the jombies disappeared. The Furious Five and Shifu were left stunned.

Back at the Jade Palace, Shifu found a scroll written by Oogway. Shifu read Oogway's words:

I was an ambitious young warrior leading a great army. Fighting by my side was Kai. My closest friend. One day we were ambushed. I was badly wounded. My friend carried me for days, looking for help. Until we came upon a secret village high in the mountains, where pandas used the power of chi to heal me. Kai realized that what could be given could also be taken.

Oogway also described how Kai began stealing chi from the pandas. Oogway realized he had to battle his best friend.

Our battle shook the earth until, finally, Kai was banished to the Spirit Realm. Should he ever return to the mortal realm, he can only be stopped by a true master of chi.

Shifu and the Five were wondering about the best way to handle their new foe when Li turned to Po. "I can teach you the powers of chi, but you have to come home with me to the Panda Village. You have to learn what it is like to live like a panda, sleep like a panda, eat like a panda. Those 103 dumplings? I was just warming up!"

"I've always felt like I wasn't eating up to my full potential!" Po cried.

So Po said good-bye to the Valley of Peace and set off with his dad Li. But it wasn't long before Po discovered his other dad, Mr. Ping, had stowed away in his backpack. Mr. Ping explained that he was worried the Panda Village might not have the kind of food Po liked—and he would never be able to save China on an empty stomach!

When they arrived, Po couldn't believe how beautiful everything was. There were babbling streams, waterfalls, lush green trees, and pandas everywhere. It was paradise!

The pandas ran up to greet Po. Everyone wanted to give him a panda-size hug!

"He's all skin and bones," said a panda. "Didn't anyone feed you?"

"Hey!" shouted an offended Mr. Ping.

The next few days were some of the happiest of Po's life. Panda training was just what he'd always wanted—sleeping until noon, playing games, and the best part of all: No more walking down hills ever. Why would Pandas ever walk down a hill when they could *roll* down instead?

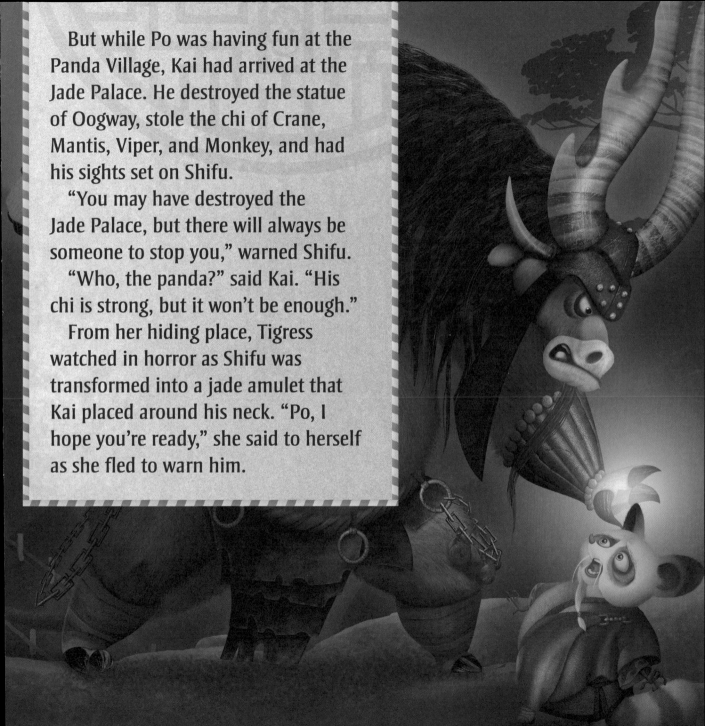

But while Po was having fun at the Panda Village, Kai had arrived at the Jade Palace. He destroyed the statue of Oogway, stole the chi of Crane, Mantis, Viper, and Monkey, and had his sights set on Shifu.

"You may have destroyed the Jade Palace, but there will always be someone to stop you," warned Shifu.

"Who, the panda?" said Kai. "His chi is strong, but it won't be enough."

From her hiding place, Tigress watched in horror as Shifu was transformed into a jade amulet that Kai placed around his neck. "Po, I hope you're ready," she said to herself as she fled to warn him.

Before long, Tigress had made it to the Panda Village. "Kai's on his way here," she announced. "He's after you, Po. He's after all pandas."

Po turned to his dad Li. "Teach me about chi now."

But then Li shocked Po by admitting he didn't know the chi technique! He only said he did so Po would come to the Panda Village, where he would be safe.

Po decided he would defeat Kai using the Wuxi Finger Hold he had used to defeat Tai Lung. But Tigress told Po he would never get close enough to Kai. Suddenly, Po saw his dad Li and all the pandas standing behind him.

They all wanted to help.

"We can be just like you," Li said.

And that's when it hit Po like a dumpling to the head. "I don't have to turn you into me. I have to turn *you* into *you*!"

Po helped fine-tune what the pandas were already good at, like catapulting, kicking things, and twirling ribbons, only now the pandas would twirl nunchucks!

When Kai and his jombies arrived, the pandas were ready for them. Their mission? To distract the jombies until Po was close enough to Kai to stop him with a Wuxi Finger Hold.

"Belly gong!" Po's cousins shouted as they smooshed Jade Crane between their bellies.

Smaller pandas rolled into the jombies like bowling balls taking down pins.

Big Fun stopped Jade Monkey with a big hug!

Mei Mei and her friends used their nunchucks to take out the Jade Badgers.
Li and Mr. Ping formed a double-dad defense and dropped Jade Shifu to the
ground.

From the sidelines Kai watched it all. "Stop! Stop! Enough!" he cried out.

Po turned to him. "Let's finish this," he challenged. He leaped up in the air,
aiming right for . . .

Kai! Now Po could perform the Wuxi Finger Hold. The battle would soon be over.

"Skadoosh!" shouted Po in triumph. But nothing happened.

"Did Oogway teach you that little trick?" Kai taunted. "Too bad it only works on mortals, and I am a Spirit Warrior!"

Energized by Po's failure, Kai and his jombies came back stronger than ever.

"You really thought you could send *me* back to the Spirit Realm?" asked Kai as he closed in on Po. Soon he would have Po's chi and then the chi of everyone else in the Panda Village. Po knew he had to do something.

"You're right," he told Kai. "I can't *send* you there, but I can *take* you there!"

Po jumped up and landed on Kai's back. But this time he didn't try the Wuxi Finger Hold on Kai—he did it on himself!

Kai and Po were blasted into the Spirit Realm. But Po was still no match for Kai with all his stolen chi. Things were looking bad for Po as Kai began turning him into a jade amulet. Suddenly, from the mortal realm, Li realized that he could still reach Po. He gathered all the pandas, and they sent their chi to him. In the Spirit Realm glowing paw prints appeared on Po's chest! The pandas in the mortal realm were passing their chi to Po.

Beautiful gold beams radiated out of Po.

Po looked up. The gold beams had turned into a huge, glowing dragon of chi.

Kai was shocked. "A dragon?" he gasped. "Who are you?"

Po wondered for a moment how to answer. Who was he? The son of a panda? The son of a goose? A student? A teacher? In a flash he realized he was *all* these things. "I am the Dragon Warrior," Po proclaimed proudly.

Po channeled all his chi and the chi from all the pandas directly at Kai. It was too much for the Spirit Warrior. He was defeated. And with his defeat, the jombies were freed!

Having defeated Kai, Po was pushed back into the mortal realm. When he opened his eyes, he saw his two dads staring down at him with pride.

"We thought we lost you," said Li through tears of joy.

"No, you saved me," said Po. "You *all* did. The students truly became the masters. Thank you."

It was time for everyone to return to the Jade Palace. And that's just what they did . . . including the pandas of the Panda Village. And the Valley of Peace was never the same—it was way more awesome!